You Can Swim, Jim

You can Swim, Jim

Kaye Umansky & Margaret Chamberlain

RED FOX

SPLASH! Whoopee! Hey, look at me!
I'm first one in, the water's fine!

Sam don't howl. You've lost your towel?
Never mind, I'll lend you mine.

Jilly says she's feeling chilly.

Clive can dive. Look! There he goes!

Come on in, Jim. You can swim, Jim.
Take a jump and hold your nose.

Look at Jeannie's
wee bikini.
That looks lovely.
Is it new?

Sore eyes, Doreen?
That's the chlorine.
Goggles
are the thing for you.

Clark has got a rubber shark
(A birthday present from his gran).

Don't look grim, Jim. You can swim, Jim.
You can swim, you know you can.

Kate does handstands underwater.
Wow! That's great, Kate, we're impressed!

Lola's lying on her lilo,
Says she needs a little rest.

Gail's pretending she's a whale.
Watch her do a water-spout!

Come on in, Jim. You can swim, Jim.
Come on in, don't hang about.

Walt is swimming underwater.
Says he is a submarine.

What d'you say, Fay? Hip hooray!
They're turning on the wave machine!

This is what I call a giggle!
Hold on tight now, everyone.

Will you come, Jim. Don't look glum, Jim.
Come on in, it's so much fun.

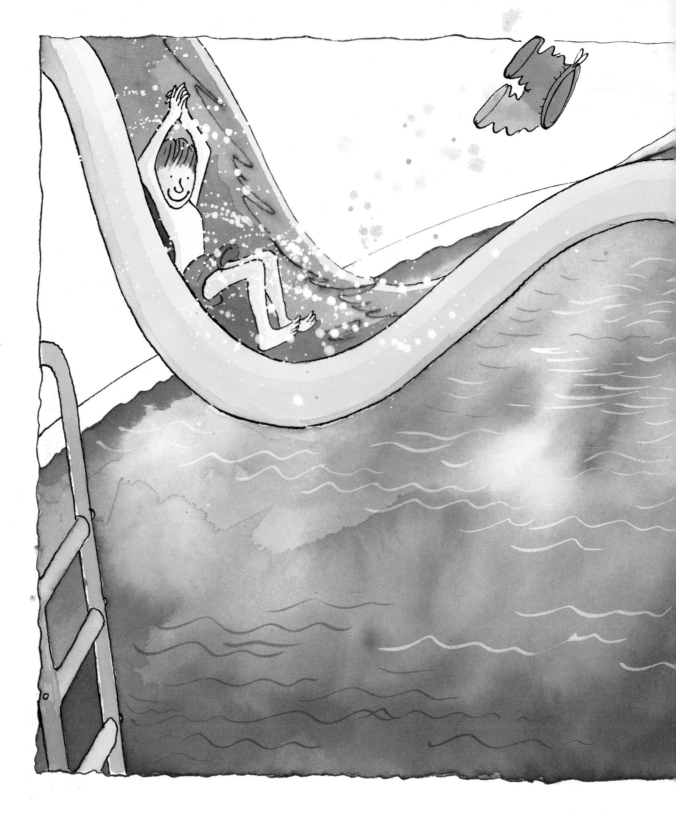

Brad's gone mad! He's up the ladder!
Now he's sliding down the chute!

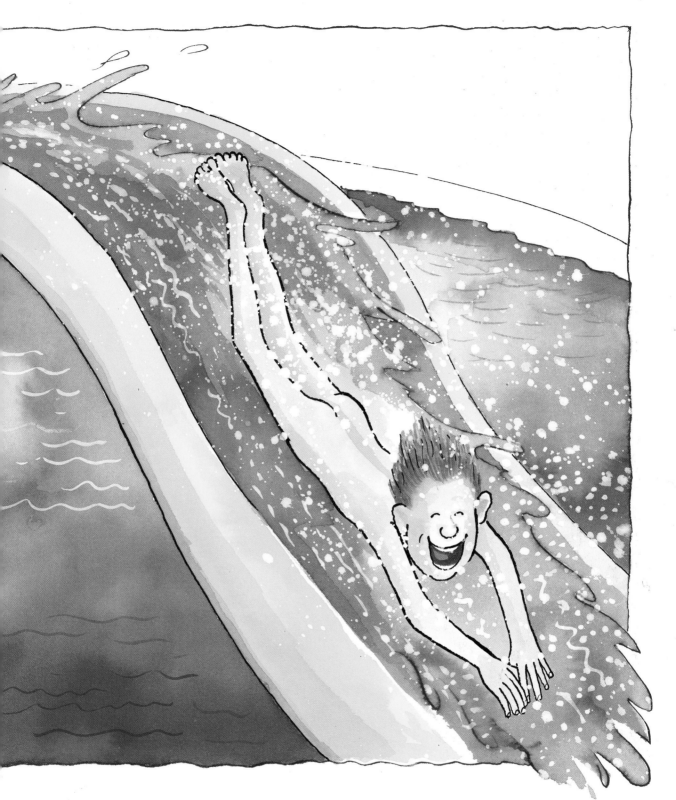

That was speedy, yes indeedy.
(Shame about his bathing suit.)

Jim looks grumpy, gone all humpy.
Says he doesn't want a dip.

Going off to buy some biscuits –
Mind, it's slippy! Jim don't trip!

SPLASH! He's fallen in the water!
What a great catastrophe!

Jim's in trouble! Lots of bubbles!
Where's he gone? Oh deary me!

Up he bobs and look, he's smiling!
Hey there, you lot, watch him go!

You can swim, Jim! You can swim, Jim!
You can swim! I told you so!

A Red Fox Book

Published by Random House Children's Books
20 Vauxhall Bridge Road, London SW1V 2SA

A division of Random House UK Ltd
London Melbourne Sydney Auckland
Johannesburg and agencies throughout the world

Copyright © text Kaye Umansky 1997
Copyright © illustrations Margaret Chamberlain 1997
Designed by Rowan Seymour

1 3 5 7 9 10 8 6 4 2

First published in Great Britain by
The Bodley Head Children's Books 1997

Red Fox edition 1998

Printed in Hong Kong

RANDOM HOUSE UK Limited Reg. No. 954009

ISBN 0 09 966941 2